This book belongs to

....

My favorite shape is

....

For our boys, William and Sam.

First American Edition 2021
Kane Miller, A Division of EDC Publishing

Text © Naomi Jones 2020
Illustrations © James Jones 2020
The Perfect Fit was originally published in English in 2020. This edition is
published by arrangement with Oxford University Press.

For information contact:
Kane Miller, A Division of EDC Publishing
5402 S 122nd E Ave
Tulsa, OK 74146
www.kanemiller.com
www.usbornebooksandmore.com

Library of Congress Control Number: 2020936318

Printed in China
2 3 4 5 6 7 8 9 10

ISBN: 978-1-68464-141-3

THE PERFECT FIT

Naomi Jones   James Jones

Kane Miller
A DIVISION OF EDC PUBLISHING

This is Triangle.

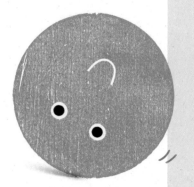

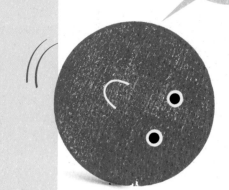

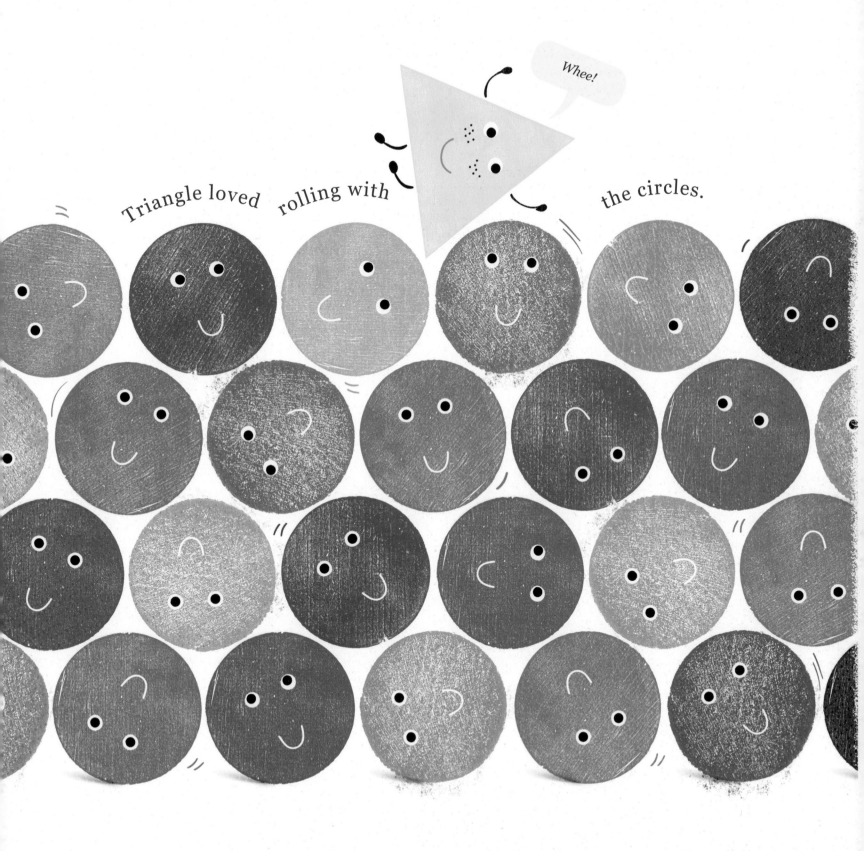

But sometimes she felt a bit *different*.

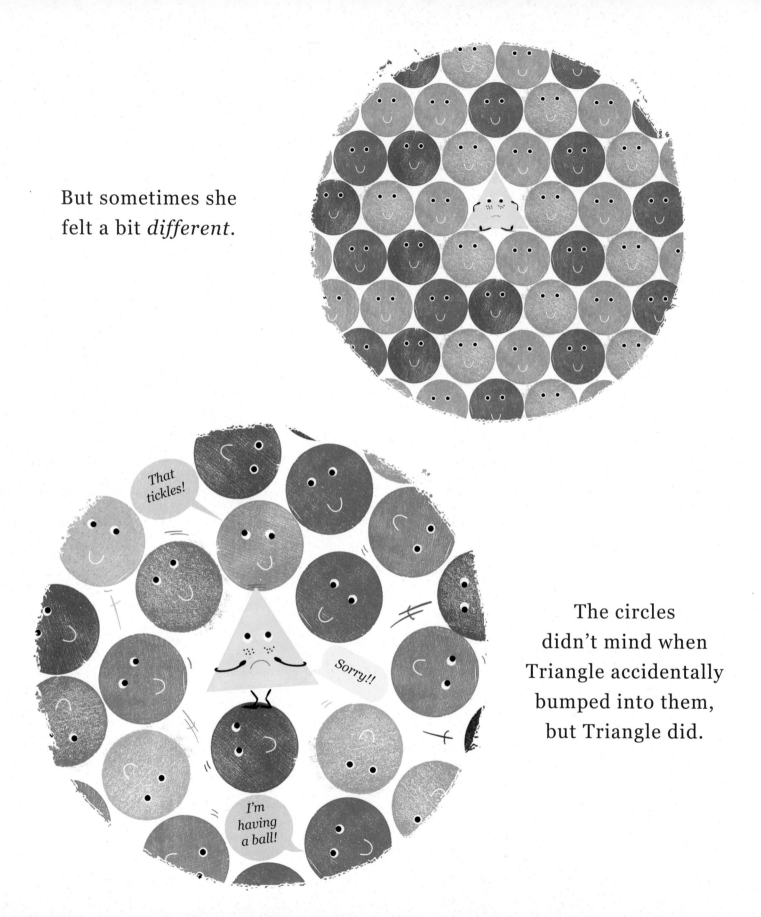

The circles didn't mind when Triangle accidentally bumped into them, but Triangle did.

Stick around!

She felt
like she
was getting
in their way.

Oh dear . . .

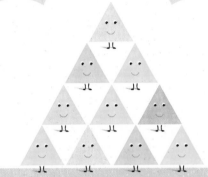

So she decided
to find somewhere
she could truly belong.

"Come and play with us!"
the squares said.

So Triangle did.

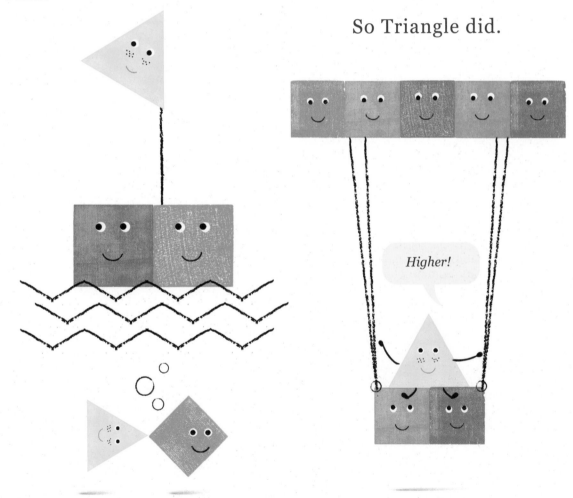

They played all sorts of games and it was terrific.

"Let's build a tower!"
one of the squares suggested.

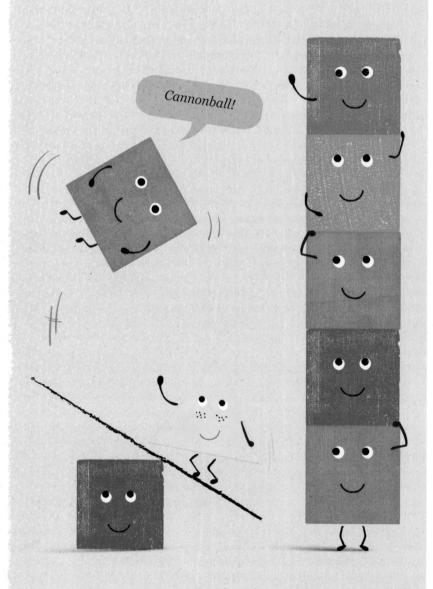

So Triangle
hopped up
to help,

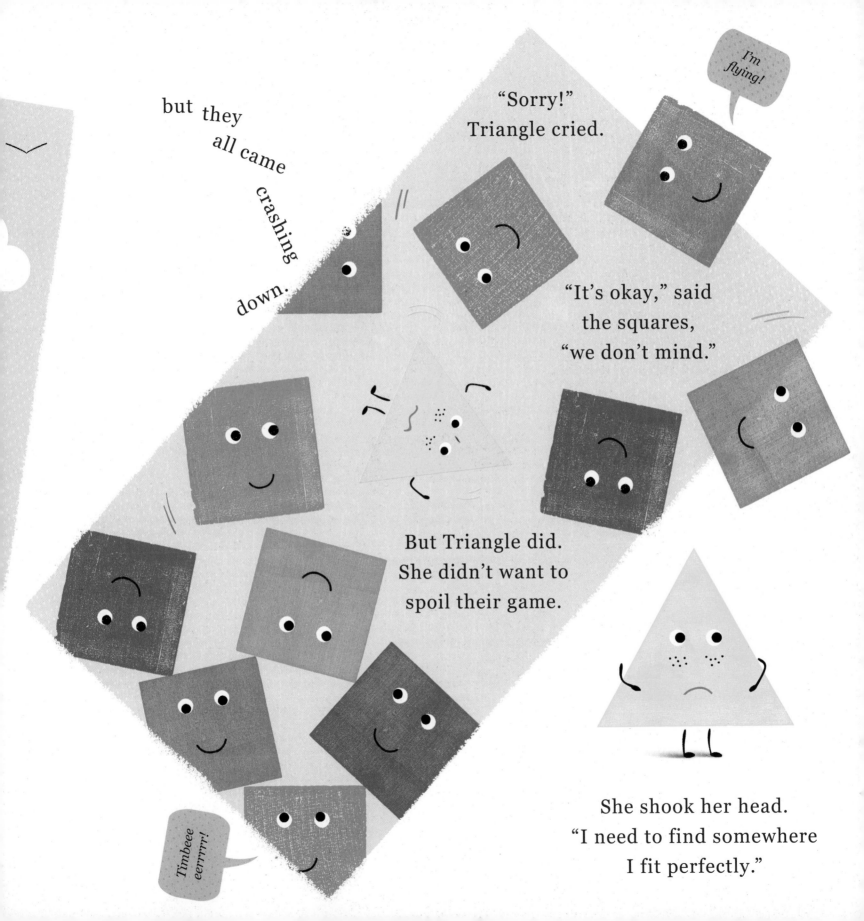

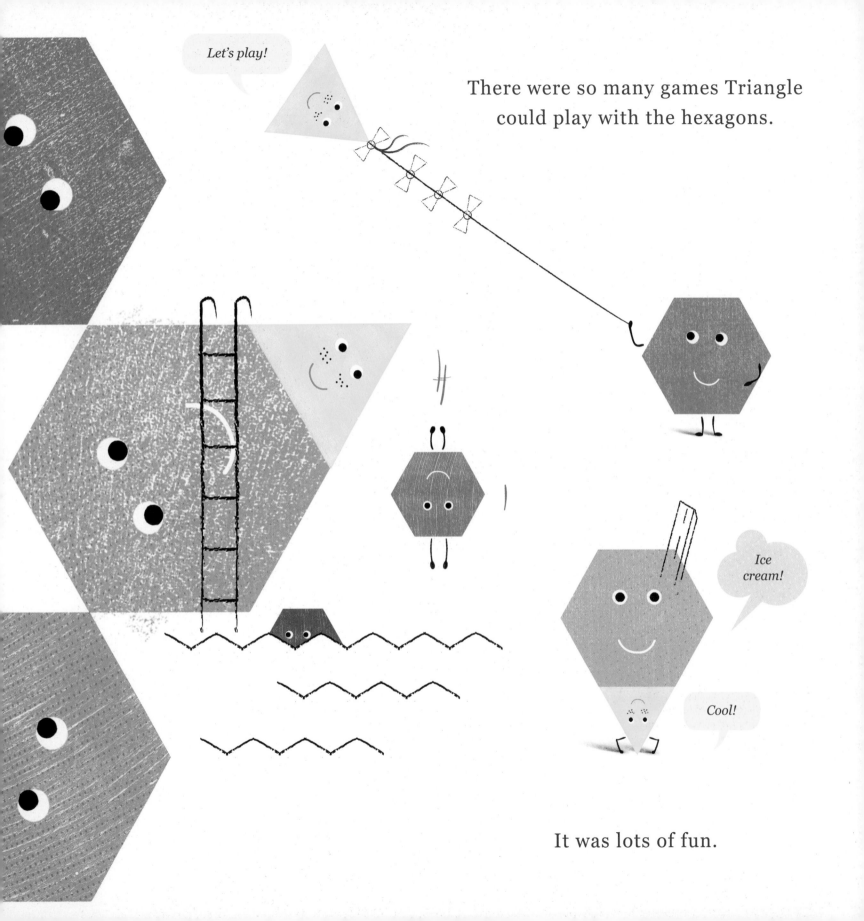

There were so many games Triangle could play with the hexagons.

It was lots of fun.

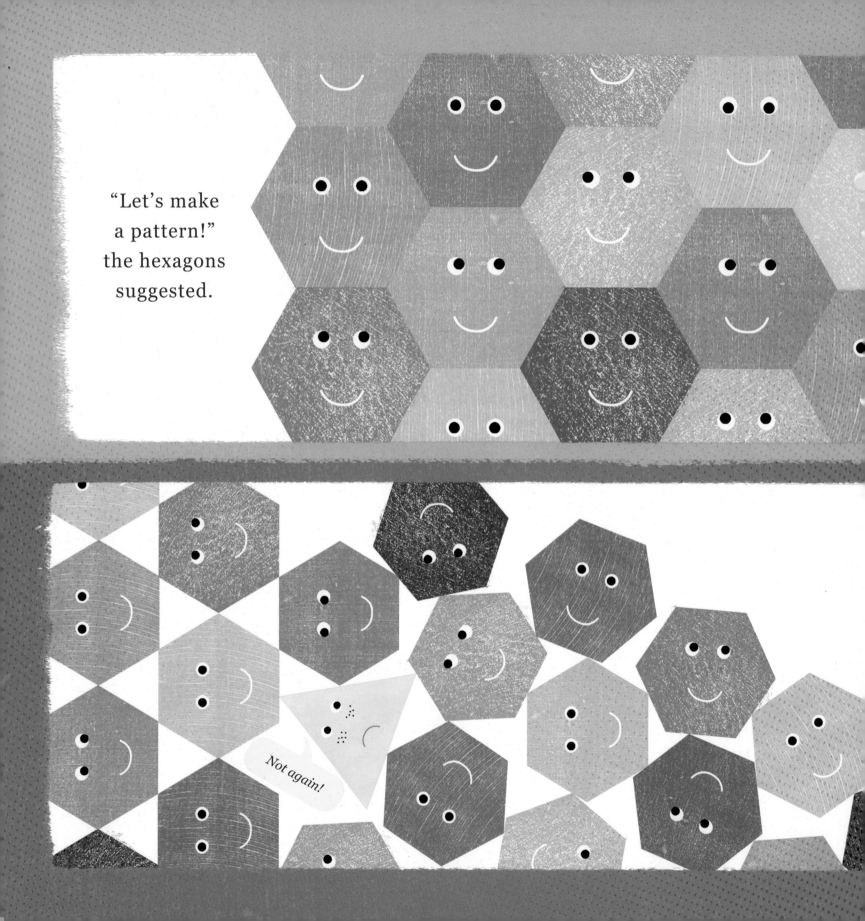

"Let's make a pattern!" the hexagons suggested.

Not again!

Triangle joined in, but she kept making the pattern *different*, not the same.

"We can play something else," the hexagons said.

But Triangle decided to say goodbye and keep on going.

Triangle searched
and searched . . .

but couldn't find anywhere
she fit perfectly.

She was starting to
feel very fed up.

"Maybe there aren't any other triangles.

"Maybe I'm the only one?"

But then she looked up and thought she saw a familiar shape in the sky.

"You're not a triangle are you?" Triangle asked.

"Almost—
but not quite!"
the star said.

Triangle sighed.

"Don't worry,
there are shapes
that look exactly
like you and they're
not that far away . . ."

Finally
she found
them. Triangles
that were exactly the
same as her, in every single
way. She rushed over to join them.

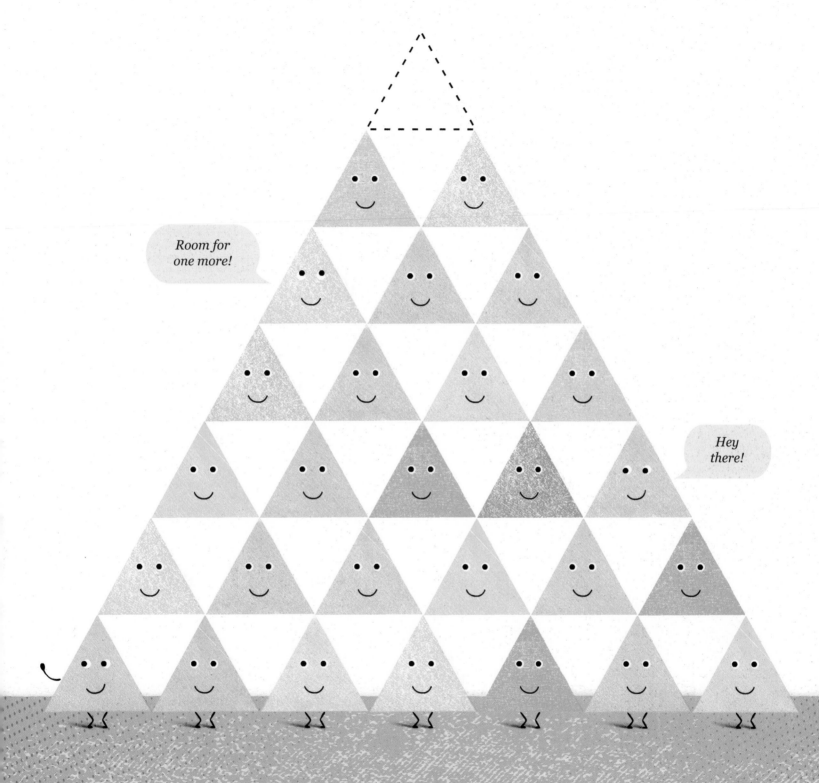

Together they played
lots of triangle games
and it was wonderful.

"What shall we do next?"
one of the triangles asked.

"Let's roll!"
Triangle suggested.

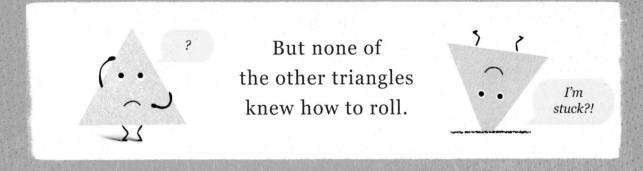

But none of the other triangles knew how to roll.

As Triangle tried to show them, she thought about all the fun she'd had with the other shapes and it gave her an idea.

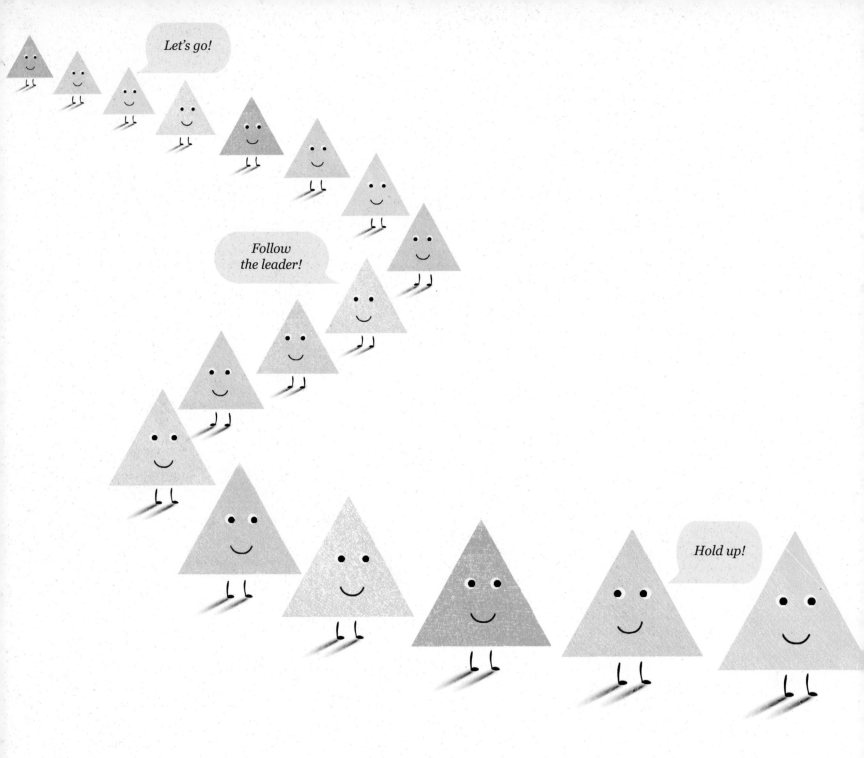

"You found
the others!"
the star
called down.

"I did," Triangle replied,
"and we had lots of fun.
But I realized there was
something missing . . .

everyone else!"

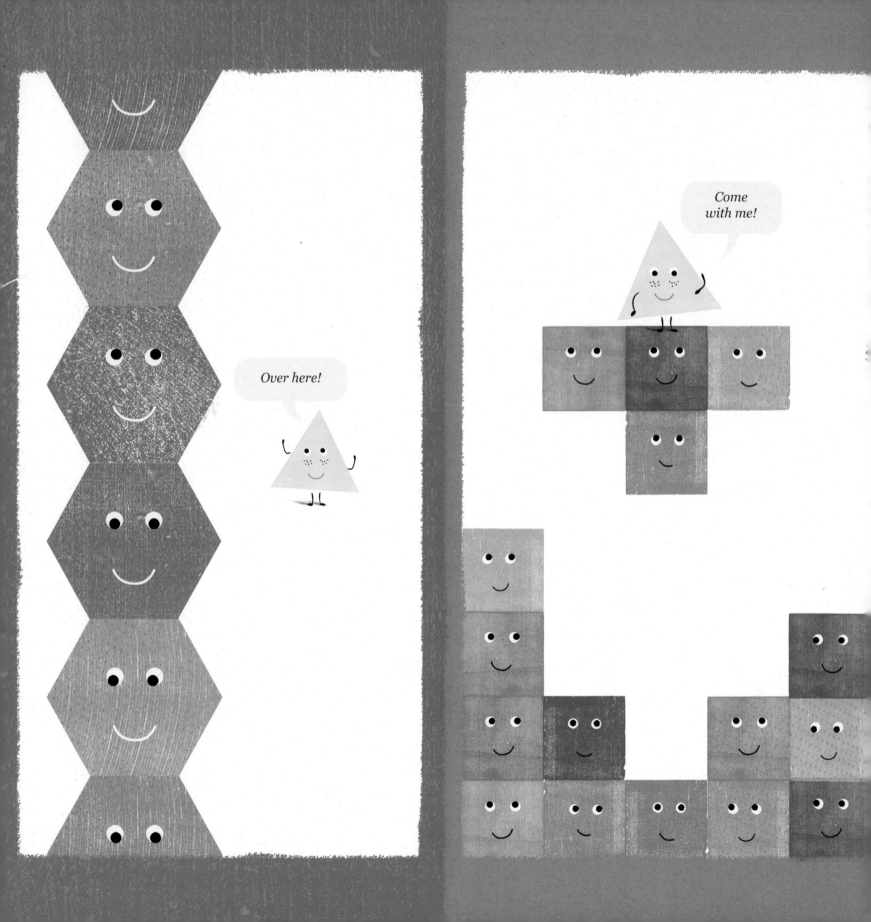

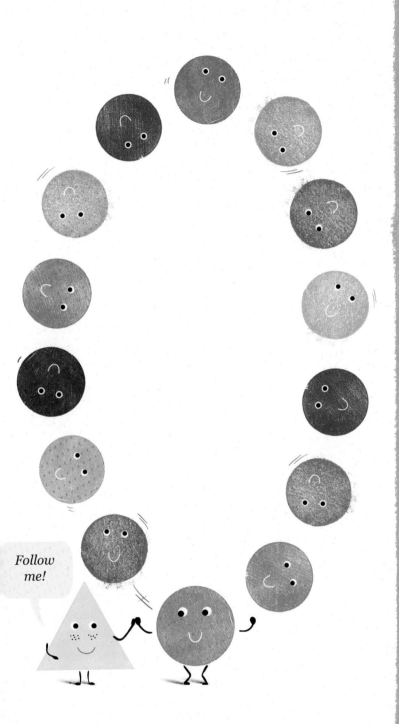

Follow me!

"I used to think that I didn't fit in with shapes that weren't like me. But then I realized how much fun we're all missing out on by not playing together.

So, would you ALL like to play with me?"

The shapes were very excited.

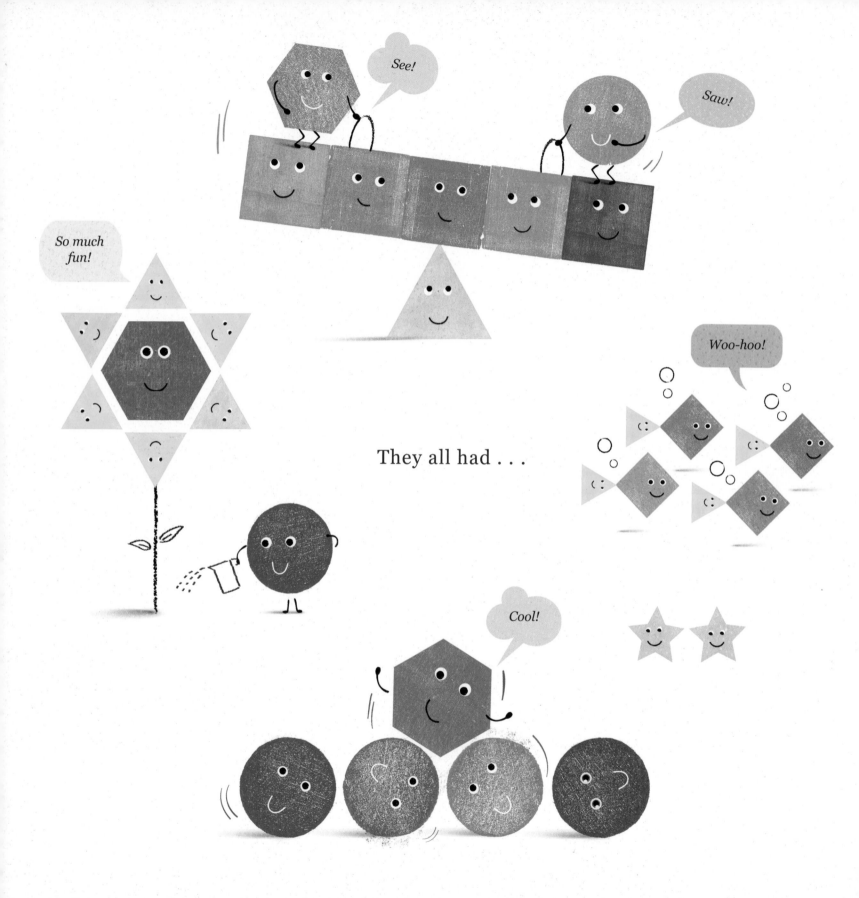

They all had . . .

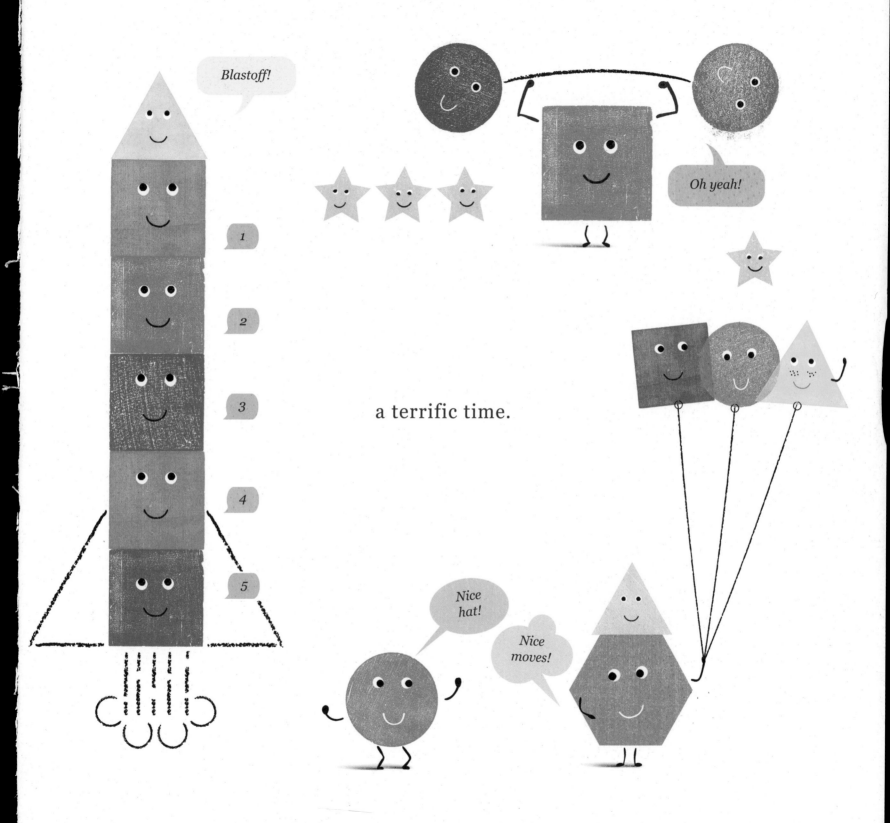

a terrific time.

And even though

Triangle wasn't exactly

the same as everyone else,